Faerie Blood

Jeremy Berg

Faerie Blood

Copyright © 2013 Jeremy Berg

Edited by Aidan Spangler

Book Design and Illustrations by Jeremy Berg

Published by Lorian Press
2204 E Grand Ave.
Everett, WA 98201

ISBN 10: 0-936878-63-0
ISBN 13: 978-0-936878-63-8

Berg/Jeremy
Faerie Blood/Jeremy Berg

First Edition: June 21, 2013
Printed in the United States of America

www.lorian.org

Dedication

This book is dedicated to Kendall O'Brien who first introduced me to the delicious joys of being a grandpa and to Delaney, Aiden, David, Persephone and Xyla Mae who each in their unique way introduce the experience anew in surprising and wonderful ways.

Acknowledgments

My appreciation and gratitude to:

John Matthews, who allowed a fledgling Lorian Press to publish his book on the Sidhe. Without his book this book would not have been created.

David Spangler, who has been my teacher and collaborator in many explorations and I am proud to call him friend.

Freya Secrest, my lovely partner, who has the unenviable task of reading and commenting with tact on all my first drafts.

My editor Aidan Spangler, who made this book as good as I would allow.

RJ Stewart, who has been holding the faerie tradition true for many years and has my deep respect for his work.

Adrienne McDunn for her unflagging support.

And to the Sidhe of Scotland whose story formed the seed of this story.

To one and all thank you.

I am a grandfather now. It seems like such a short time ago I was young – barely a teenager – and sitting at the bedside of my own Grandpa. We both knew he was dying. He was happy to talk about it. I couldn't bear the thought. But there we were in his bedroom late at night. The full harvest moon staring at us through his open window. The light fall breeze ruffling the curtains. The Doppler whistle of a distant train heading west barely audible. He in bed propped up with three pillows. I on his big armchair pulled up close, holding his wrinkled, weathered hand. His gold wedding band grown several sizes too big on his shrunken ring finger. Grandma had died years before and everyone else had gone home for the night to frantically catch up on their lives. My parents let me stay. Everyone had accepted the inevitable except me. We were alone.

All the smells come back to me now. The slightly antiseptic too sweet waft of failed medicine. The untried beef barley stew on the bed-stand. The faint background swirl of decaying fall leaves. The cut flowers left by well wishers. His body odor from the last several days in bed. *Winter's coming.*

The sounds are there too if I choose to remember. His raspy breathing, the ancient oil furnace chugging along almost imperceptibly in the background. The call of a night owl, just once the whole night. His big, wind-up, pocket watch ticking away on his dresser.

And the taste of salty tears.

The whole night is there etched in my bones as if engraved in headstone granite.

"You know you have faerie blood," he said quietly, breaking a long silence. As if this was the most common comment to make for a man who made his living as a stone mason. A decorated veteran who fought in the trenches hand to hand with a bayonet. A smart, tough, wizened, dogged man. An honest, down-to-earth man's man.

Here we go, I thought. He's slipping into the shadows and mists where I can't follow. I had overheard my aunts talking once about him a couple of years ago. They thought he was already 'getting senile' and 'seeing things that weren't really there' but he always seemed as solid and rooted as a big old oak to me.

"Don't go Grandpa", I said, "not yet, don't go." I had heard the whispers from the adults all day long. He could go at anytime, the hospice nurse had said.

"Don't go where? Where do you think I'm going? I'm not dying this precise moment," he chuckled, then coughed and tried to hide the cough with another chuckle. He had a great laugh and a quick wit and an earthy, raucous sense of humor. I miss that about him.

"What did you say, Grandpa? I know this sounds crazy but I thought you said we have hairy blood!" I tried to make it sound like I just wasn't hearing him properly.

"Be quiet now, son," he said gently. But he could be stern at the same time, and he was being so now. "I have a story to tell you and maybe not enough time left to tell it. This little episode came on quicker than I expected, and I need to complete my obligations to the old ones."

The "little episode" was a severe heart attack. They found other things when he was admitted to emergency. Terminal, he said when he told us, but not serious.

"I wanted to wait a couple of more years before laying all this on you but my heart beats to its own drum, I guess."

And then, as if on cue, he writhed, clenched his jaw in pain, clutched at his pajamas with his free hand and crushed mine with his other. Then his grip went slack and clammy. He was panting and sweating and his rheumy eyes looked glazed and unfocussed.

I didn't know what to do. "There is nothing you can do," my dad said to me when he left for the night. "If you insist on staying the night, understand that he could easily die right in front of you. You need to be prepared for that if it happens and let him go!"

So I just sat there staring at him, holding his wet noodle hand for what seemed like an hour at least. It was probably ten minutes.

He was looking away when he spoke again, barely audible. "He's very young and not yet ready."

"Were you talking to me, Grandpa," I said under my breath, relieved that he was talking at all.

No response for another minute or two and then he asked with a weaker voice but as if nothing much had happened, "Where was I?"

"You said something about old ones, Grandpa." The phrase had stuck sideways in my mind all through his episode, looping in the background. I was intrigued but worried he was losing it, and I, him.

"The old ones ... that's what I call them. The Faeries, the Sidhe, the Tuatha de Danann. You know, Tolkien's Elves! I know you have an interest. I see it in you. It sometimes skips a generation or two but it always seeds, sprouting from the family tree. It's landed on you big time, so you need to carry it through to the next generations. I'm about done – ready or not."

He said this with such gravity and finality and acceptance that I held my breath for several counts then breathed out with a snuffling sound.

"You sound like a horse," he laughed. "I said you had faerie blood, not equine!"

"OK, Grandpa, if you say so." I had decided to humor him. No sense arguing with a dying man.

"Don't humor me." he retorted. "If you think Elvis has left the building, just say so!"

I never could put one over on him very well.

"It just seems a little far-fetched." I swallowed hard. "You know, fairies and gnomes and all. Ever hear of fairy tales, Grandpa? It means it's not true or just a myth."

"I didn't say anything about gnomes, but if you want to talk about them, I guess we could."

I could tell he was baiting me. Humoring me. Biding his time for me to approach the subject head on. There was no time to bide.

I tried a different approach. "OK, tell me about the faiiiriies." I strung out the word to let him know the entire conversation was his idea.

"Why do you have all those books about them?" he smiled. "It worries your mother a bit you know. She thinks you're a little strange … just like me. She never liked my spiral tattoo."

"You, Grandpa? How could she think you were strange? She's your daughter."

"Well, children think what they like about their parents," he said, "Nothing you can do about that but be the best father you can be."

This was the Grandpa I knew. Giving sage advice to a young man struggling to become an adult ... like him.

"But really," he continued, as if this were just another summer conversation on the back porch swing at the cottage, "why all the interest in pre-Celtic history? What do you think drives your fascination with Stonehenge and the standing stones and the 5,000 year old barrow at Newgrange?"

"You know about those?" I asked, a little surprised. This was something we had never talked about before.

"I was in Europe, you know, during the war to end all wars. And I visited there a few times afterwards. I was looking up at a Tiffany stained glass window of the archangel Michael, and someone appeared behind me. Something about that image resonated with the world of Faerie." His voiced trailed off. "That's where I first started to work with them more actively."

"Work with who?" I was beginning to feel like I was in the twilight zone. My eyelids began to feel heavy, and I wondered whether I wanted to stay awake much longer. He had been sleeping off and on all day while I had exhausted myself pacing around and worrying. Perhaps I had already fallen asleep and was dreaming.

"Come on! You know who."

Nope, unfortunately I was still awake. "But they're just a myth like a fantasy story from Charles de Lint. I like to read about them, but they're not REAL. Fairies are like angels, dragons, unicorns, or flying horses. You know, made up, imaginary, fantasy."

"Speaking of dragons . . . . . ," he left the word just hanging there.

"Grandpa!" I said, exasperated. Then lowered my voice. "Grandpa, you know what I mean."

"Yes, I do," he said slowly. "But do you? Myths are often rooted in facts, and imagination is more than you think it is. What stories do you think ancient peoples told about dinosaur bones? Do you think it is possible that with the stone bones of a Tyrannosaurus Rex, someone might have decided that some really big scary creatures lived somewhere or sometime? Or how about the fossil of a Pterodactyl?" He was quiet for a moment, catching his breath. "They weren't dinosaurs you know but pterosaurs." he said parenthetically. "You know some had wingspans of over 18 feet? Maybe these are your dragons ... or not. Maybe there are dragons."

I rolled my eyes and looked around the room. We were in his private area. His bedroom. Someplace I rarely went. I was struck by the number of books he kept. Shelves and shelves of them. He wasn't highly educated or anything – just high school – but he was a scholar in his own way. Always reading stuff. Always up to date. Always making me think for myself with his questions. Always throwing in odd science facts. He was always teaching, even now with his last breaths.

"OK, OK," I relented, "Some stories are real ... or start real anyway. But **fairies**?"

"Well, you have to make up your own mind about them, that's for sure. But as a man I expect you to face new experiences with courage even when they are strange or unpleasant," he said with emphasis.

I blushed, and my chest tightened with pride. He had called me a man for the very first time. I held back another round of tears.

"Go to my closet," he said. "Over there." He barely moved his hand to point. "On the upper shelf is an old wooden box with brass hinges. Bring it here."

I did as he had asked. Opened the closet bi-fold door by pulling it towards me, then felt around for the single bare bulb's pull chain. I remembered hiding there once when I was a little boy, playing hide and go seek. I felt shivery and deflated knowing I may never see the inside of this space again. I wanted to just shut the door and stay there next to his clothes and shoes and travel bags. The signs of his life. I found the light and reached up to the shelf. It was too high, so I looked around for something to step up on.

"There's a stool in there," he called, anticipating my problem, "on the right, inside the door."

I found it and stepped up and rummaged around. There was only one box of that description, and I was soon back at his bedside. He had pushed himself up a bit, apparently with some effort since he was breathing heavily and looked flushed.

"Open it," he instructed. "Turn on the overhead light and hand me the stuff inside the box."

Grandpa turned even more pale and grey in the harsh light. "Can we just use the nightstand lamp, Grandpa? I like it better," I said mildly, not wanting to draw attention to the way he looked.

"No problem. Maybe it's better that way," he said. "The Sidhe are luminous enough for themselves."

He never talked down to me. I liked that about him even if I had to look up words later.

The simple weathered wooden box had a worn brass latch but no lock, and it opened smoothly – like it had been used quite a bit over the years. I handed him the contents. There were two items immediately apparent: the first was a large flat greenish stone pendant sitting on top. Under it was a leather bound book with a clasp that looked like a worn old photo album. It had a silver rose in the upper left hand corner. That's why the box felt so heavy. I picked up the stone and felt a strange sensation run through me, as if I were imbedded with deposits of iron and the stone was a magnet. Then the feeling was gone.

"These go way back," he said. "Matter of fact, that stone you're holding dates to a time before written history – at least in Europe. I was told it was from the Isle of Iona … off the coast of Scotland. You know, where Columba made his church in the sixth century AD. But this stone is much older than that. Well, of course the stone is old. Iona has very ancient exposed rock. But what I mean is that the carving is very old."

"How old?" I asked. Then I stopped and wondered. "Who told you?"

"That is a great question. Now we're getting to the heart of the issue. The answer is my great grandmother. Your great, great, great grandmother. Her name was Fiona O'Cairen"

"She sounds great," I joked.

"Very funny. Maybe you inherited the defective pun gene too." He laughed softly, then his voice stiffened. "But I'm serious. Look at the carving in the stone. This was made centuries ago … by one of your distant ancestors."

He left the last statement dangling in the air like a fishing lure. I knew I was the fish.

The rock was etched or carved and worn smooth by many hands. It had a clear carving of a spiral with a line through it.

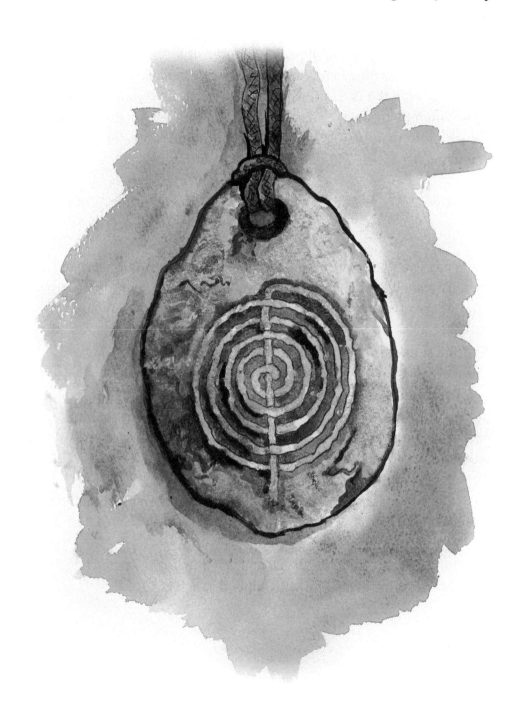

"What's in the leather book?" I asked, taking it out of the box. Underneath there were also a couple of other smaller metallic pendants. I took them out and laid them on top of the album. "What's with the jewelry ... and why the silver rose?" He seemed more alert and keen on this subject so as strange as it was I was ready to encourage him.

"The pendants were worn by other members of our clan as a reminder of Faerie. They're yours now," he said, but did not elaborate. "In our family and in some of the old tales, the silver or white rose has been a symbol of the Faerie worlds. Humans are sometimes represented by a red rose. I guess because we have iron in our blood to make it red. You know, the hemoglobin which carries oxygen?" he added, throwing in an odd fact.

I nodded my head to say I had heard of hemoglobin and iron in our blood. I put the album and the jewelry on the carpet by my chair and pushed them away with my foot so Grandpa couldn't see.

I was trying to create some distance between the old stuff and me. At this stage I was pretty convinced that Elvis had left, in spite of the box and its contents. All they proved is that he had a weird collection and maybe he was batty all along.

"I'm not sure if their blood is white, or of this is just legend. They're of a different substance. Maybe this is why some say our Faerie Kin are allergic to iron. But don't accept everything you hear. There's a lot of nonsense said about the Faerie worlds."

"They can appear looking rather silvery," he added, as if remarking about the color of one of his old Harleys.

"Along with the stone pendant, this album holds the records of the carriers of this family tradition. Great grandma O'Cairen introduced me to the family tradition with this album, so maybe I'll start there with you too."

It was strange to hear my Grandpa talk about his great grandma. I tried to picture him as a boy but came up blank.

"How old were you then?" I asked.

"About 21, I guess. It was a long time ago. She wasn't dying when we had this talk, but she was in her 90's. Back at the old farm. In a rocking chair knitting most of the time or just looking out the window.

"She was fun to talk to, though. Wonderful sense of humor. Really could tell a story. She had sparkling, sky blue eyes just like yours. Then I was off to the war and never saw her again except in visions and dreams." Grandpa's voice trailed off. "I can almost hear her voice . . . ." He seemed far away.

"Grandpa?"

"Oh, right. Where were we? You visited the old family farm didn't you? Down by the river … looking out to the mountains."

"I think we drove by the land once but never stopped. It was full of new houses."

"Progress!" he huffed. "I loved that old place and now it's gone. But maybe something better is coming." he added.

"Better?" I asked. I was still holding the stone and running my fingers over the carving.

"That's what this whole Faerie thing is about, you know, something better for you and for the world." He paused. "Sorry, I'm getting ahead of myself. Let me start where all good legends begin."

"Where's that, Grandpa?"

"Why, at the beginning of the world, of course," he said, smiling.

I settled back just like when I was a small boy on Grandpa's lap and he was going to read me a story. I could almost smell the lingering aroma of his pipe tobacco. He might be nuts but he always could spin a good yarn.

"A long time ago when the earth was young and still gathering the life forces and primal materials from asteroids storms," his voice began to sound as if he were reading a scroll behind his closed eyelids. "Then Gaia, our mother earth, saw the need in the distant future for a special kind of life to join forces with her. Among the trilobites that roamed the ancient seas, her plans for bees and trees, and all the other wonderful evolutionary experiments, she wanted humans to add their nature to her biosphere. She invited our deepest ancestors, the proto-humans I call the Starwizards, to build a home with her.

"We had and have something essential to bring, a special creativity, our unique song to add to her melodies of joy, dancing and singing around the sun." He stopped. "You know the sun was about 25% cooler when the earth was formed about 4 1/2 billion years ago?" he asked.

I waited. I didn't know that fact but wondered if it was relevant to the story. Grandpa had a tendency to diverge at the best of times. And this was not the best of times.

"The point is that we were invited here from the cosmos..."

"You mean, we came here in space ships, like ancient astronauts," I interrupted. This wasn't quite as far-fetched as fairies but it was still pretty far out.

"No, no. I'm talking about spirit, son. We came as spirits from...well, who knows from where...the old lore says from the cosmic realms of spirit." He shook his head. "It doesn't matter from where. The important thing is that Gaia wanted us to contribute something to her project."

He clenched his fist and shook it in irritation. "All this talk about humans being a blight on the earth, a cancer? Phooey! It's just nonsense! How could a being of such majesty and intelligence make such a mistake. How could she help evolve a life form over millions of years that she didn't want?" He hesitated. "Although we do some pretty stupid things sometimes."

"I guess," I said, not wanting to interrupt.

"When did this invitation happen and when did we arrive?" Without waiting, he answered his own question. "I don't know. Let's see. Organic life began on earth about 3 1/2 billion years ago, there was an explosion of multi-cellular life around 530 million years ago. Mammals were around with the dinosaurs after the Permian extinction 245 million years ago.

"Many people don't know that." he said parenthetically, "They think mammals out-competed the big clumsy dinosaurs, but nothing could be further from the truth. Dinosaurs were the dominant life forms until a huge asteroid wiped most of them out around 65 million years ago.

"All we have left of them are the birds. The first primates came later, about 50 million years ago. Perhaps that is about the time humans arrived."

"I don't think so, Grandpa," I interjected, partly to stop the lesson in evolution, partly to let him know that I had been reading too, and partly to keep us connected to reality. "Primates that walked on two legs came about 7 million years ago not 50." Early bi-pedal primate evolution was a favorite subject of mine since I did a paper on it for science class.

"Very good" he said. "You've been studying."

I beamed .... then my stomach clenched. This is what made it hard to believe Grandpa was dying and crazy. His voice and mind were sharp and clear. Everything seemed normal when he talked. How could death be so close? My darkening thoughts were interrupted as he continued.

"What I meant was that we arrived in the etheric regions of the earth. this is the non-material part of the earth that influences the physical parts that we normally see." He emphasized the word normally. "There are lots of names for it, but I've always been fond of etheric."

"The etheric, Grandpa?" We were back in the netherworlds.

"Yeah, just think of it as a catch all word for all the otherworlds and forces that you can't see but know are there. Like magnetism and mathematics and memory."

"Like ghosts." I said. Then realized that I had put my foot in it. I didn't want to talk about dead people.

"Something like that," he said with no apparent worry about the subject, "But ghosts who never had a body like ours. Think of us as if we were born living in the ocean and never saw the shore but there are

all these other species that live on land and fly through the air. Whole ecologies. We never see them unless they wade into the water, or we jump out but they are part of the whole cycle of life on the planet and affect us in many ways. We could not thrive without them or they without us."

"If you say so, Grandpa." I relented.

"Trust your own feelings and follow the facts," was all he said. I squeezed his hand in acquiescence, and he squeezed back, looked at me kindly and continued.

"Anyway, at some point a long time ago, the starwizards started to influence a branch of primate evolution we now call hominids. Maybe that is what triggered primates to diverge from other mammals. I don't know, but at this time long ago – to use my metaphor – all proto-humans lived on land and in the air and had just put our toes in the ocean."

He stopped and breathed repeatedly in and out rapidly, almost panting. He seemed to be out of breath and his skin was blotchy. But when he started up again, his voice was strong.

"We are an imaginative species." He said. "That was as true then as it is now. We love to think outside the box as they say, create and play with new ways of doing things. Perhaps that is one of the reasons Gaia wanted us here. This shows quite early in the archeological record. Stone tools have been found that are at least 2 1/2 million years old. I think they were called Oldowan tools by Leaky because of the region of Tanzania where they were found."

"They sound old." I smirked. "like Oldo Wan Kenobi from Star Wars."

He groaned. "Oh no, it's true. You *have* inherited my pun-gent genes," throwing one in himself.

It took me a minute to get the pungent reference but then I laughed and groaned right back.

"That was a good one, Grandpa," I said, "but stinky!" This is another thing I miss about him. His quick wit and terrible puns.

He chuckled, then furrowed his brow in concentration. When he did his hand began to shake and his whole body began to shiver. I knew he was hanging by a thread.

He took several shallow staccato breaths, then continued.

"So, long ago – whenever this was is not important – some part of humanity began a project of creating a living world within a world. Sort of an artist's community; painting and sculpting with the underlying formative life forces of plants and animals that were already firmly established in the physical parts of the earth. They built a genuine garden of Eden and experimented with cooperating with various species to bring forth new combinations in the etheric worlds. Or so the story goes.

"This garden had its own natural boundaries as all gardens must and became exquisitely beautiful.

"They were working with time differently than we do. They're able to mold it and shape it somewhat to their bidding. So they could influence evolution somewhat like we might do with genetic engineering." His voice quavered a bit.

"The difference is they were working directly with the intelligence of the species with their full cooperation." He cleared his throat.

"This is what the Findhorn community in Scotland began to do in the 1960's. You may have heard of them." He shuffled around apparently trying to get more comfortable. "There are books out about Findhorn and the people who started it."

"Can I get you anything Grandpa? Water, another pillow, juice or something? Is the light OK?" Truth be told I was a little lost.

"Everything's fine," he said. "I'm just old and creaky. Nothing we can do about that right now."

He finally seemed to get his body into a comfortable position and continued. "I think this may be where some of the stories of dragons and unicorns and other mythical creatures come from," he said almost under his breath, as if he were talking to himself. "I once had a dream that felt very real, with a solemn troupe of several others riding grey

Pegasi, winging down a misty river in the twilight. It had the feel of the Fey otherworlds now that I look back."

"Fey?" I scrunched up my nose. "What are Fey?" I was hoping this didn't lead into a whole new weird line of discussion.

But he just said, "Oh, you know, just another term for the Sidhe."

"Shee," I responded. "Are they all females?" I was trying out the word for the first time, and my teenage brain was picturing a world of beautiful, long haired, buxsom girls with bows and arrows riding white unicorns in rainbow meadows. I rather liked the image, especially the way they were dressed.

"It's spelled S-I-D-H-E," he said slowly, "but pronounced Shee. It's Gaelic for people of the mounds or hollow hills. And no, they are not all female – sorry. There are men and women and children in lore and in my encounters, although I am told they rarely reproduce."

This was mildly disappointing to me for some reason.

Grandpa cleared his throat, then began coughing in short grunts, sounding as if he had swallowed something gooey and it was stuck.

I started to get up but then he grabbed his handkerchief with his free hand and spit something slimy into it.

"I'm OK," he croaked. "Just needed to clear my gizzard."

"Humans don't have gizzards, Grandpa, chickens do."

"Are you calling me a chicken?" he chuckled, feigning indignation.

We were back on track, and he seemed to be out of this latest crisis.

"Wouldn't dare," I said playfully. "You're bigger and stronger than me." In the past, this was always true, and I wasn't ready to give up the illusion just yet.

"Give me some water will you?" he asked, sounding rather weary.

I handed him his glass, and he took a sip and gave the glass back for me to return. "Where was I?"

"You were talking about a garden," I reminded him. He nodded as he picked his story back up again.

"So you can see that there was a time when all humans – what I called the starwizards or proto-humans – were one integrated race. Gradually, though, the differences between those in this artists project and others of the race started to emerge. A fundamental disagreement arose when some of our kind wished to remain immersed in the fluid etheric realms while others felt drawn by the challenge of new frontiers, wanting full embodiment into blood and bones.

"All were aware of the dangers to our quicksilver nature of complete identification with the crystallized elements of the earth. Many were equally aware of the profound experiences that could be had if we could forge an alliance between our fluid natures and physical matter. Some felt that the crafting of this alliance was the essential reason we were invited to the earth in the first place from our other cosmic homes."

He stopped.

"That is a mouthful, Grandpa. I'm not sure I understood much of it," I admitted.

"That's OK. The bundle of stuff in the journal contains several versions of the story written by some of our long lost relatives and some photos and things I put in there. You can read it later when you feel up to it. Take good care of the bundle as some of the paper is fragile."

He looked intently into my eyes.

"You don't need to follow everything I'm saying. Just sit back and try to get the overall thrust of the story. Think of yourself as a sponge, and you're absorbing only as much water as you can hold right now. Let me finish the tale and then we can talk."

He cleared his throat several times and began again. "Choice is fundamental to being human, and in the end there was no way we would all agree. So, for some brave souls the migration into matter began. I think this might be when the first bi-pedal primates began to appear. But I'm not sure. This event might have been much later. And anyway, the separation probably wasn't a single event but rather a gradual drifting apart of the two factions over a long time."

I interrupted. "So let me get this straight. Millions of years ago our planet earth, who is a really a big somebody named Gaia, asked some kind of hyperdimensional humans to come live on earth from somewhere out in space. Some of the humans stayed up in the "cloudy mountains" making beautiful gardens and became faeries, and some came down to the earth and made mammals into primates and then into us. Is that about right?"

"Hyperdimensional, I like it. Where did you get that term?" Grandpa asked with a slight smile. "So much for letting me tell the whole tale." he added wistfully.

"From a comic book," I said reluctantly. "That's where I got the idea."

"As good a place as any, I guess," he said seriously. "You know a lot can be learned from fiction and fantasy. And, yes, you have it about right."

"This all sounds pretty crazy," I said. "Do we have any proof?" I was getting a little irritated at Grandpa, and at myself for feeling this way.

I hoped it didn't show.

"Proof of the pudding is in the eating," is all Grandpa mumbled before starting up again.

I decided to humor Grandpa by treating all of this as a fantasy novel or comic book story. I didn't want the irritation to get the better of me, especially in these circumstances.

"After the split began," he continued, seemingly oblivious to any doubts I was having, "many on both sides of this developing divide turned their backs on the other and went about their lives, ignoring the others. However, many on both sides continued to engage with each other, albeit increasingly in constrained and restricted ways.

"The way these two factions of humanity interacted with each other over the many millennia is long buried in the swamps of history. We do know, however, that during large gatherings, the gateways between the fluid and fixed worlds were held open by elders of both races who stood in a great circle overseeing the event.

He pointed to the album on the floor. "As you'll read in there, our family's story, though, picks up after the last ice age in Europe.

"Around that time, the engagement between Sidhe and human took the form of grand festivals – fantastic trade bazaars that were magnificent happenings when the pathways between the worlds were opened and for a limited time everyone traveled freely from one realm to another.

"Great standing stone circles were erected to create the dedicated space and safe boundaries for the festivals. There were thousands of major and minor locations for these gatherings as shown by the remnants of stone circles or henges like at Mayburgh, Avebury, Callanish, Stonehenge and the like.

"Each stone was erected as a kind of magical talisman and linked to an an elder who was capable of surrounding and saturating the stone with qualities of life-energy needed to sustain the connection between the worlds and among the participants of the festival. The individual standing stones were linked together in the circles, sometime with overhead lintel stones like at Stonehenge, and the circles themselves were linked with other similar circles throughout Europe and the world.

"I am told that linked together by earth energies, the various circles of standing stones acted as a kind of communication network, even facilitating travel between them at great speed. The technology of these circles is lost to us now, but one can still feel the resonance of power at the ruins of these sites.

"I hope you get to visit some of these sites," he said, changing the cadence of his 'story' voice.

"Anyway, during the solstices and equinoxes and at other special times of the year, the Sidhe would arrive with a theatrical flurry; the

women dressed in their finest shimmering gowns wearing intricate jewelry and the men decked out in polished silver and gold armor over form-fitting fabrics, carrying light ceremonial weapons. The humans greeted them with a colorful fanfare of feathers, feast and fire.

"It is from this era that the stone pendant you hold originates and our family lineage with the Sidhe begins. Young people, being what they are, facilitated a certain amount of mingling of the white blood line of the Sidhe and red blood line of Humans during these times, if you know what I mean," he said with a wink.

I blushed just a little. "I know what you mean, Grandpa."

"The story passed down in our family is that one of these festivals was on the Isle of Iona off the western coast of Scotland. There's still the remnant of a Cairn and stone circle there near what is now called the Hermit's Cell. It's at the base of a rock formation that resembles a huge lion.

"Hand me the album. There's a photo of that place I took in the late 40's somewhere in here." He opened the leather bound records and began leafing through. He gave it back opened to an old photo. "You can just see the remnants of the ancient Cairn in front of the rocks."

I turned the book sideways and looked at the old photo which had tinted with age. I could imagine my Grandpa taking this picture. On his dresser there was a framed picture of him with grandma on vacation

around that time. He loved to hike in wild places.

"Getting color pictures was expensive then," he said, "but I felt it was worth it. Everything was expensive in Europe right after the second war to end all wars." There was a tinge of sadness in his voice but without commenting further he returned to his story.

"The pendant you hold is about 10,000 years old and marks the birth of a little girl who was the result of the love between a Faerie father and Human mother. The stone with the carved symbol was given to the mother by the daughter's Sidhe grandfather. He was one of the Elders who wore the cloak of the stone. By concentrating on the carved symbol they could visit with the father and his family whenever they wanted. It still works that way."

"Wow, 10,000 years old!" I was a little blown away by the date. This was almost as old as the first cave paintings. "It must be worth a lot."

"It is," Grandpa said, "but its value is not measured in money."

He fumbled with the top button of his pajamas with trembling fingers.

"Where was I?" he said to himself. "Oh yes. Over the millennia, the requirements of entering deeper and deeper into physicality for humans and the increasing insularity of the Sidhe from the rigors of that same physicality began to create misunderstandings at these events and even occasionally a previously unheard of scuffle or argument.

"Then disaster struck. Some say it was a disgruntled father fresh from a boar hunt catching his only daughter in the arms of her ethereal lover. Others say it was triggered by a slight given to the Queen of the festival. Whatever the initial spark, a conflagration followed. As I said, the Sidhe had weapons too. Their realm is not without natural dangers and conflict. During that period of our history, many of our kind proudly carried sharp wooden spears and flint knives and bows and arrows which that day were beautifully decorated for the festival but deadly nonetheless. The day ended with the commingling of white and red blood in ways not meant to be.

"When kin battle kin there is nothing more anguished or horrifying. Some say the standing stones themselves curled over in grief or crashed to the ground or cracked wide open.

"Needless to say, the elders of the two "cousin" races soon concluded that the cyclic festivals could not continue in the same way.

"Contact between our peoples from then on was strictly limited from both sides to seers, shaman, bards, priests, healers and the like. The Sidhe withdrew into their more etheric domains – what we quaintly call the Hollow Hills – and we dove deeper into ours.

"The extravagant festivals gave way to shorter Hollow Hill days mediated by trained officiates. Over time the origins of these holidays were mostly forgotten, and that which was once a human treasure was interred in the sediment of countless years of sifting time.

"However, a truth cannot be fully buried, and there remained and remains to our current time a residual awareness of a primal connection to each other, to otherworlds and to the etheric parts of the whole human organism. To this day there is a large man made mound near Wiltshire, England called Silbury Hill which I sense contains an active Sidhe memorial to this event. It is in view of the West Kennet Long Barrow which is a human burial chamber."

"Grandpa"

"Yes"

"I have a question." I was hesitant to ask but forged ahead. "I can see that you believe this right now – and maybe all of this is true – but why does it matter?"

"Now that, my friend, is a really wonderful question! And, I might add, diplomatically put not to call me senile."

I sputtered, he laughed. I also heard him call me friend and tucked the memory away in a safe place to savor later.

"It matters because both races, Human and Sidhe, are reaching a dead end. I'm sure you don't need me to tell you that our species faces big problems; nuclear war, pollution, overpopulation, you name it. And who knows what you will face in the new millennium. But it is also true that the Sidhe are stuck. They hold a powerful vision of our place in the cosmos, but they also live in a kind of bubble world of their own imagination. It is like a star-lit world of mirrors, and they need to reconnect with us to break out of their own reflections. Together we might be able to figure out how to survive and thrive on this beautiful planet. Healing the ancient split could help create a whole new civilization. A world of hope and promise."

"Yes," I said. "I worry about what we're doing to the environment."

"You should. It shows you have a good mind and heart. But never give up hope. There are resources available to us in the realms of spirit that we have only just begun to tap. We are here to bless the earth and each other and ourselves. Sidhe and human need each other to reach our full potential." He paused, then added, "And speaking from experience, faerie muses can help you in your life in surprisingly useful ways." His mysterious smirk reached all the way to his eyes. "Count on it."

It felt like he had finished. I had nothing further to say and no further questions to ask. I just sat there trying to absorb his story and store it in a place where it could sit comfortably. I found no such place. It was too strange. So we sat together without speaking for quite some time.

"It is time," he said like an iron bell tolling.

My heart sank. "Time for what, Grandpa?" I managed to squeak through tightening jaws.

"Time for you to make a decision," he continued in his commanding tone. "Whether you want to take on this mantle of the family's work. It is your choice. It will always be your choice from this time on 'till the end of your life."

"But what is this mantle, Grandpa? What is the family's work?"

"It's what I've been talking about, keeping alive the relationship with our inner cousins, the Sidhe. It's a work of helping the two sides of humanity become whole again."

"What if I'm not ready?" I inquired, hesitant to accept anything which might make Grandpa feel done with his work. I was pretty sure I was NOT ready for anything this crazy, so I was stalling.

"You'll know if you're ready. And, whether you're ready or not, it is time for me to complete this task. Do you know what a ritual is?" he asked. "Or a ceremony?"

"Like in a church?" I asked, "Or a wedding or something? Or do you mean a magical ritual with candles and weird symbols? There are lots of those in movies and in some of my books."

"Something like a combination of all of those," he said, "except no candles or scary symbols. Just think of it as a time of focusing, of bringing your full attention to all of the life around you and within you. Think of all the wonderful skills and talents you have. You have a good mind and a loving heart and a strong body and a lively imagination. I am proud of the man you are becoming!"

This was the second time he had referred to me as a man, and it felt just as warming.

"Let a feeling of gratitude wash over you about the wonderful home you have and the good things of life. Now just take a minute to look around this room. Look at the details. Really pay attention to it. Appreciate the craftsmanship, the wood floor, the drapery Grandma made, the windows, the chair you are sitting on, my bed. Feel the stone foundation connected to the ground it sits on and the yard outside. Let it help you connect to the land around the house and to the earth."

This seemed harmless enough.

"Now remember some of the good times we've had together. Let that feeling link you with the rest of the family and with our ancestors. I know there have been problems from time to time but feel the undercurrent of love that everyone shares in this family, what bonds us. Think of one of those lazy times when we were fishing or something that makes you feel good. Think of your friends and imagine them as part of the whole human family."

"My friends will think I'm crazy if I tell them this stuff." I muttered.

"Quiet. Just listen now. Don't worry about your friends. That will work out fine just like it has for me. You don't need to tell them anything you're not comfortable sharing."

His voice had adopted a kind of rhythm which was both soothing and seemed to resonate with overtones of distant music just out of earshot.

"Close your eyes, feel the weight of your body in the chair, listen to your breathing."

I slumped in my warm chair. My head nodded. I felt the sandman coming.

"Make a picture in your mind of something like Stonehenge or Clava cairn but simpler. It is surrounded by a primal forest that goes on forever beyond an open meadow. There is a light, warm summer breeze and you are alone walking into a grassy meadow under a blazing, star-lit sky. In the open space is a wide circle of very weathered, massive standing stones, each bigger than a tall man and wider. Some are covered with moss and some look like they have carvings which you can't quite make out in the twilight. Some are leaning a bit but all seem to be pulsing slightly, almost breathing. It feels like the forest is full of animals and creatures which are coming close to our circle to watch and listen.

"Some of our ancestors who have carried this work over the centuries are stepping out from the woods into the clearing. Some are men and some are women. They appear dressed in the clothing of their time–from deerskins to ruffled dresses. Some of the pendants and jewelry they wear look familiar. Their faces are intent and solemn but kindly too.

"The Sidhe draw near and stand with our ancestors. One ancestor and one Sidhe stand on each side of every stone in the circle."

Suddenly I found myself actually standing a little above the grassy meadow at the edge of the forest, bright starlight shining down on a circle of big standing stones. In the center was a large mound of stacked rocks of varying sizes. Facing me in the distance was an entryway made of two wide, upright stones about crawling height with a block of stone sitting over them forming a doorway.

I was awed by the blue black sky with countless stars sparkling above me and, oddly, stars also blazing from within the stone doorway of the cairn. I felt a warm breeze. There was a thick, inviting smell of lavender in the air.

I began to walk down the slight incline. The path led around the inside edge of the circle to my right and spiraled around toward the middle of the circle in front of the opening. Each stone seemed to have a personality all its own, with a faint glow of silvery light pulsating from it and around it. They seemed to bow slightly and acknowledge me and whisper, but I couldn't understand the language or hear them clearly as

I walked.

A powerful voice filled the bowl of the stone circle vibrating right down to my bones. "Will you stand with us? Will you hold with us the ancient gift of humanity to the earth? Will you weave and wear with us the cloak of remembrance and tell a new story of humankind? Will you let a new heaven and a new earth be born in you?"

I really didn't understand all the voice was asking or many of the implications, but something welled up within me at that moment which felt fully right and completely natural. "Yes!" I responded. "I will do what needs to be done and what I am capable of doing to bless our earth."

Looking back I wonder what gave me the confidence to do what I did and the words to say what I said. But when I completed my statement, the stones all began to glow even brighter and then to dissolve. Their light surrounded me, and I felt myself standing in the circle as one of them – one of the stone guardians, capable of helping to sustain the circle. Then, in place of the stones, the Sidhe and my ancestors, stood a circle of very beautiful, very tall men and women dressed in flowing shimmering pastel hues of silvery light. They felt like family.

At the center of our circle in the place of the Cairn stood what I can only describe as an angel of the earth radiating a green tinted light which surrounded our circle and lit the primeval forest beyond. "I accept your gifts," she seemed to say, "and offer you my blessings in return."

"How are you doing?" Grandpa intruded softly. "You've been gone awhile and I'm wondering if you're OK."

I was back in my familiar chair by the bed. My heart was thumping, my mind was swirling and my body seemed to have been plugged into some electric socket somewhere along the line. "Wha ... what just happened, Grandpa?" I stammered.

"Something wonderful." he said. "Something you won't soon forget if you're anything like me."

We sat quietly for a long time. He seemed to be holding my hand now to keep me in the room and bring me back to my normal state. "Breathe," he would say from time to time, "just breathe."

Gradually I realized Grandpa had not squeezed my hand for well over an hour. The only movement was the slight rise and fall of the thin blanket with his shallow, ragged breathing. I began to hold my breath with each of his ... waiting between the lengthening intervals. The day seemed to be dawning early as a soft light suffused the room. But then, strangely, the light seemed to condense around a tall, diffuse silvery figure on the other side of the bed holding Grandpa's free hand. It looked like he was sculpted from moonlight. Oddly, I felt no fear but rather gratitude that someone had come to help.

"He's leaving now," the mercurial glow seemed to say. His voice flowed like tumbling rocks in a mountain stream. "Would you like to walk with him awhile to his new home?"

While I was by no means sure what this meant, I certainly wanted to be with my Grandpa, so I nodded my head, YES.

Suddenly, Grandpa sat straight up in bed and looked at me squarely in the eyes and squeezed my hand hard. He turned toward the figure, smiled, then fell back with a long sigh.

Immediately, I found myself walking hand in hand with my Grandpa along a worn stone path. He seemed spry and healthy and energetic. We approached an old stone foot-bridge with a blue-black river rushing underneath.

"Where are we Grandpa?" I asked. "This looks like a bridge you could have built."

"We all build this bridge when we have to," he said and laughed. "But we get a lot of help. Thanks for yours!"

It felt peaceful. It was a comfortably warm, sunny day and the fall colors were in full bloom on the opposite shore. There were rich organic smells carried across on the slight breeze, reminding me of Grandma's garden when I was really little.

We walked slowly up the incline of the bridge, stopped and stood together at the top.

"I need to go on the rest of the way alone," he said quietly, letting go of my hand. "You have been a wonderful companion and I appreciate all you are to me. Remember our time together tonight."

He gave me one of his big muscular hugs. "I love you very much."

Then, just as suddenly as I had whisked away, I was back in Grandpa's bedroom.

"He's gone," said the shining figure, "but never really very far away." The figure was becoming more transparent as he spoke and soon seemed to be just the first light of morning filtering through the drapes.

I was alone, and Grandpa's body was still.

My forearm began to itch, and as I pulled up my sleeve to scratch, I noticed it. A small, blue spiral tattoo had appeared on my arm just like one grandpa had had. How would I ever explain that!

The End

Epilogue

As I said at the beginning of this story, I am a Grandpa now too. It is drawing near to a time when I need to pass this family mantle to my grandchildren and theirs. So I guess this story will go into the old, wooden family box along with all the other mementos, letters and notes, and pictures and pendants.

And perhaps it is time for this work to spread beyond our family. Perhaps it is time for all of our kind to find kin in the realms of Faerie.

Further Explorations

The following materials can be found
at www.lorian.org in the Bookstore

The Sidhe: Wisdom of the Celtic Otherworld
by John Matthews

This popular book wraps a fascinating tale around John's connection to the Celtic otherworlds. Through his conversation with the Sidhe deep insights into the Faerie realms are brought to light. The book is full of wisdom and interesting detail about this "cousin" race to humanity. It includes six exercises and a tool of contact with the Sidhe called the Great Glyph. 120 pages plus Preface. $15.00

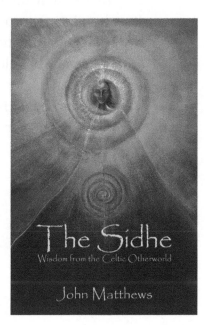

The Great Glyph Silver Charm

This silver charm of the Great Glyph which was introduced by John Matthews in his book *The Sidhe* measures just under ¾" in diameter. It is a shimmering reminder of our connection to the Celtic otherworlds. $12.00

Card Deck of the Sidhe

By David Spangler/Art by Jeremy Berg

In 2011, David Spangler and Jeremy Berg had independent but related contact with a group of Sidhe interested in promoting closer contact and collaboration with human beings. One result of this contact was the creation of the *Card Deck of the Sidhe*.

The *Card deck of the Sidhe* is composed of 33 full color, premium 3.5" X 5" cards in a fabric carrying pouch and a 188 page manual outlining meditative, storytelling and oracular uses of the cards. It comes packaged in a sturdy box with a clear lid and full color box sleeve for long term use. $33.00

A Midsummer's Journey with the Sidhe

By David Spangler/Art by Jeremy Berg

This FULL COLOR book is a magical journey into the realms of the Sidhe, the graceful "People of Peace" who are the overlords of the Faerie Kingdoms. With beautiful full-colored illustrations by Jeremy Berg and text by David Spangler, this is a journey not only into a mystical realm but also into the potentials of the human spirit and the possibilities of a new consciousness within humanity. This book contains 90 pages. *Please note that this book uses the images of the Card Deck of the Sidhe and duplicates a story in the manual.* $18.95

Memoirs of an Ordinary Mystic
by Dorothy Maclean

Dorothy Maclean may call herself an "ordinary mystic" but in fact she has had an extraordinary life with an equally extraordinary impact. This outstanding memoir tells the exciting story of her journey from being part of the British secret service during World War II to co-founding the fabled Findhorn Foundation spiritual community in northern Scotland and subsequently becoming a spiritual teacher much in demand around the world for her down-to-earth insights and wisdom. Her work with the inner forces of nature is of seminal importance in our age of global climate change and environmental challenge, offering hope for our future. Told with honesty and modesty, it is the record of one of the most significant and loving spiritual figures of our time. $17.95 - 264 pages 6X9 book with extensive photos

About the Publisher

Lorian Press is a private, for profit business which publishes works approved by the Lorian Association. Current titles by David Spangler, John Matthews, Dorothy Maclean and many others can be found on the Lorian website www.lorian.org.

Lorian Press
2204 E Grand Ave
Everett, WA 98201

The Lorian Association is a not-for-profit educational organization. Its work is to help people bring the joy, healing, and blessing of their personal spirituality into their everyday lives. This spirituality unfolds out of their unique lives and relationships to Spirit, by whatever name or in whatever form that Spirit is recognized. For more information, go to www.lorian.org.

The Lorian Association
PO Box 1368
Issaquah, WA 98027

Lightning Source UK Ltd.
Milton Keynes UK
UKHW052150180220
358939UK00005B/59